NEW HAVEN PUBLIC LIBRARY

W9-AJP-946

媚　妹　媚　妹　媚
妹　媚　妹　媚　妹
媚　妹　媚　妹　媚
妹　媚　妹　媚　妹
媚　妹　媚　妹　媚
妹　媚　妹　媚　妹
媚　妹　媚　妹　媚

Waiting for May

Janet Morgan Stoeke

DUTTON CHILDREN'S BOOKS

NEW YORK

E STOEKE
Waiting for May /

35000093905890
MAIN

❧ AUTHOR'S NOTE ❧

I wrote this story while our family waited impatiently for over two years for Chang Hai Fan, our little girl from China. (We call her Hailey, not May, but that's another story.) From the start of the adoption process, my three sons were curious and concerned about her. They asked millions of questions. They grew impatient to see her and wistful about holding her. In their hearts, she slowly became *our* baby, even without a photo to look at or a rounded belly to touch. That was what amazed me the most and what inspired this book.

Chang Hai Fan, a.k.a. Hailey Adele Brooks, with her brother Elliott

When the boys met fifteen-month-old Hailey for the first time at the airport, a friend commented, "It was like watching someone fall in love." The best part was that it lasted beyond those first hugs and smiles. It was real.

I have changed a few of the details and combined the three brothers into one to make it simpler. But the heart of the story is a truth I was happy to learn: love doesn't need a reminder to show up, and is often there before you even see it coming.

—————— A NOTE ON THE QUILT SHOWN ON THE TITLE PAGE ——————

In China, when a baby is due, friends and family offer swatches of cloth and good wishes to the new mother so she can sew a "100 Good Wishes" quilt. The red thread used to stitch it is a traditional symbol of the connection between those destined to be together. Adoptive parents from the United States have embraced this tradition, which busies their hands with a project and soothes their hearts while they wait.

Copyright © 2005 by Janet Morgan Stoeke
All rights reserved.

CIP Data is available.

Published in the United States by
Dutton Children's Books,
a division of Penguin Young Readers Group
345 Hudson Street, New York, New York 10014
www.penguin.com/youngreaders

Designed by Jason Henry
Manufactured in China • First Edition
ISBN 0-525-47098-0
10 9 8 7 6 5 4 3 2 1

For Hailey

I know that when other kids get baby brothers or sisters, their mothers' bellies get big and they go to the hospital. But we're not getting our baby that way. We are going to get ours from China. But first, we have to wait.

Mom and Dad tell me that there are baby girls far away in China who need families, and that one of them is going to come here and be my sister. Dad says that when it's time to get her, I get to go, too!

"Can we go soon?" I ask.

"No, not soon," says Mom. "There are a lot of things we need to do first. When a baby gets adopted, the people in charge of her have to make sure that she is going to a good family."

"But we *are* a good family."

"Yes, I know, but we need to send papers that will show that to the people in China. We'll get our fingerprints taken and get copies of our birth certificates and marriage license, so they'll know who we are. And we have to fill out a lot of forms."

"Can I do some? I can write the part with my name in it."

"You are getting good at writing," says Mom. "Why don't we write to Aunt Shirley after school? We can tell her all about the adoption."

Walking to the bus stop, we hear a small noise in the bushes. It's a mother bird sitting on a nest. It makes me wonder about my little sister, far away in China.

"Who is taking care of her now, Mom?" I ask.

"She's got nannies to watch over her. They live in the orphanage with the babies, and they take good care of them."

"When will we see her?"

"Well, adoptions can take a long time, maybe even a year. We need to get everything ready, and then they will tell us who she is and everything about her."

The mother bird swoops away. We get closer to the nest, and we can see four tiny eggs, with pink speckles.

A social worker named Tricia comes to see us. Mom says she's here to ask us questions and look at our house. She will write about us in one of the papers for our adoption. I show her everything.

"My sister is going to love it here!" I tell Tricia. "Everything we have is good for babies. See, I put all my marbles up high. And we have a swing. And look, we even have a china cabinet! She will love that."

"What will she like? The teapots?" asks Tricia.

"No, it's a *china cabinet*," I say. "She'll need something that reminds her of home."

"And this is her room," I say. "It's right next to mine. That way I can go to her if she gets scared at night."

Tricia tells me that sometimes it might be hard to have a new little sister. She says, "You'll have to play by yourself more. And she might cry a lot."

Maybe she doesn't think I will like having a sister, but she doesn't know. We are going to be buddies. And it's OK with me if she wakes me up. When she cries, I will hold her. I really want a little sister.

At my checkup, the doctor notices how strong I've grown since last July. He also says that I have to get an extra shot, because we will be going to another country to get the baby.

I don't like shots. But I hold out my arm. I can be brave for my sister. I don't even cry.

Later, Mom and I get ice cream, and I find out that they don't have ice cream in orphanages. I knew they didn't have moms and dads there, but I thought they had all the other stuff.

Most of the summer goes by, and Mom and Dad are still working on the papers.

"Waiting is hard, isn't it?" says Mom. "But try to remember that she is waiting for us, too."

"Is she sad that we aren't there yet?"

"She's too little to know about us. But she is ours, even if we still don't know her name, and when they say it's time, we will go and bring her home."

I wonder if waiting is any easier if you don't know you are waiting.

Mom and Dad have to get their fingerprints taken. At the finger-printing place, they get black ink all over their hands, and they share it with me so I can make fingerprints, too.

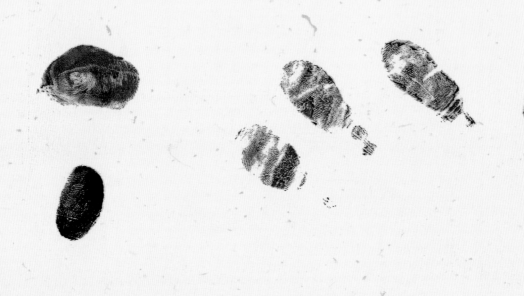

Along with the papers, we have to send some family pictures. We need one picture of all of us together. Mr. Blair is taking it. I tell him, "People in China are going to look at this picture and then pick out just the right baby for us, by looking at our faces. So could you make us look happy, Mr. Blair? And not mean. And quiet, but not too quiet. And definitely not grumpy."

"OK, I'll try," says Mr. Blair.

But how can a picture say all that? How can it show how much we think about her and want her to be with us? Can it show China how much we already love her?

We smile when Mr. Blair tells us to. And the picture turns out fine. We look like us.

Finally, all the papers are ready. We've got everything they've asked for. It's time to send them off to the agency. Then they will send our papers off to China.

"This is going to my sister!" I tell the FedEx lady when she comes to pick up the package. "Can you hurry? It's really important."

"Sure, honey," she says.

But she doesn't understand. She drives away slowly, as though she's just carrying some regular old mail.

Right after Thanksgiving, my passport comes in the mail. Dad says everyone who travels has to have a passport to get into other countries. It's like a little book. It has your picture in it, and people look at it when you get there, to see where you are from. They'll look at my passport when I get to China.

Dad says we still have to wait, because the people in China haven't picked out our baby yet. When they do, they'll send us a picture. I really want to know what she looks like.

Christmas feels funny this year. There are plenty of presents and toys and even a kitten. But I can't help feeling that there's one big, important thing missing. A sister would have been a perfect Christmas present. I wish we could go and get her tomorrow.

I name my kitten Mao. That's the word for *cat* in Chinese. We looked it up.

It has been such a long, long winter. I wonder if they have this much snow in China. What does my sister do when it snows?

"Mom, do you think she might be sad there?"

Mom says, "It's not so terrible there. The caregivers truly love the children, but they have so many babies to look after. They don't have much time for playing."

"My teacher says families in China can have only one baby. If they have two, a lot of times one of them has to go to an orphanage."

"Yes," says Mom. "There are so many people there. It's hard for everyone. I think it must be awfully hard for those mothers."

I think it must be hardest for the babies.

Daddy says when we go to China it will help to be able to say some words in Chinese. *Ni hao* is "hello," and *shye-shye* means "thank you." Chinese is hard to learn. But there's one word that's easy: *mei-mei*. It means "little sister." I could say that right away, without any practicing. At dinner, I tell everyone that I am going to call my sister Mei-mei.

Daddy says, "Why don't we *all* call her that? We could name her May and spell it the way Grandma May does."

Mom likes it, too. So now my sister has a name. And all of a sudden, she seems more real. We start calling her May all the time.

Mr. Li, one of the dads at my school, told me that *mei* can mean "little sister" or "beautiful woman." He's from China and knows how to write Chinese letters. They are called characters, and they are like fancy little drawings. He showed me what the two characters for *mei* look like. I tried copying what he painted, but writing with a paintbrush is hard.

At last I get to see May's face. The adoption agent calls and says, "Look at your computer!" The three of us stare and stare at the computer screen. They have e-mailed us a picture of a tiny girl, all bundled up in lots of clothes. Her Chinese name is Hai Fan. She has the saddest face.

All I can say is, "Look at her. Can't we go soon?"

Mom is extra quiet, and Dad just gives me a hug.

We leave her picture on the computer screen all the time. I look at her a lot. She starts to really seem like my sister after I have looked at her about a hundred times.

A week later, we get our airplane tickets to China. Dad shows me my name on the ticket. I see that it says *May* on it, too.

"Why does it have her name on it?" I ask.

"It's not her name, it's the date," says Dad. "We are going to meet May *in May*!"

"Hah! We named her right, didn't we?"

"Oh, yes. We definitely did," says Dad. "And Grandma May thinks so, too."

We pack a huge suitcase of stuff for May—diapers and toys and bottles and medicine. One bag is just presents. We will give something to each person who helps us and lots of clothes to the other kids in May's orphanage. Mom and Dad won't let me take my kitten or my remote-control car, but even that is OK, as long as we can just go!

The morning of our trip is just crazy! We have to wake up in the middle of the night, and Aunt Shirley drives us to the airport. Once we are on the plane, Mom tells me to sleep, but I can't even think of sleeping. I am so excited!

But the time in the airplane is too long. After a while, I can hardly stand it. I miss my kitten and my car and mostly my bed at home. Mom and Dad let me sleep on their laps.

Then we are there, all of a sudden, driving in a fast taxi down a busy, blurry street. There are bikes and people and cars all whirling past. There are strange food smells, and it's hot. My eyes are scratchy, and I can hardly hold my head up. But still, we are going to meet my sister tomorrow, so I can't help smiling.

It is finally time! A lady tells us that all of the babies have arrived at the hotel from the orphanage. They are waiting with their nannies in a room on the fifth floor. We go up, smiling at each other in the elevator. The elevator opens to a hallway jammed with people. Many of them are crying, but Mom says they are crying because they are happy. They are finally going to meet their babies. And the babies all cry because they don't know what's going on.

I search through the babies' faces to see if I can spot ours, but the room is too crowded with tall people. Someone says "Hai Fan," and we go over to the nanny holding May.

May is not crying but staying very still. She holds on tight to her nanny. I can tell May is scared, but brave. She stares hard at my mom, as though she can almost remember something.

The nanny talks to my parents by speaking Chinese to someone else. The interpreter tells Mom and Dad what she has said. Then they answer in English, and the interpreter says it in Chinese. It takes forever, but finally, we get to go. My mom reaches for May and holds her close. I want to hold her, too, but I wait.

We take May downstairs to our hotel room. Instead of being glad, she is mad! She wants to go back so badly, it almost makes *me* cry. We try to tell her all about how it will be at home, but she just cries and cries.

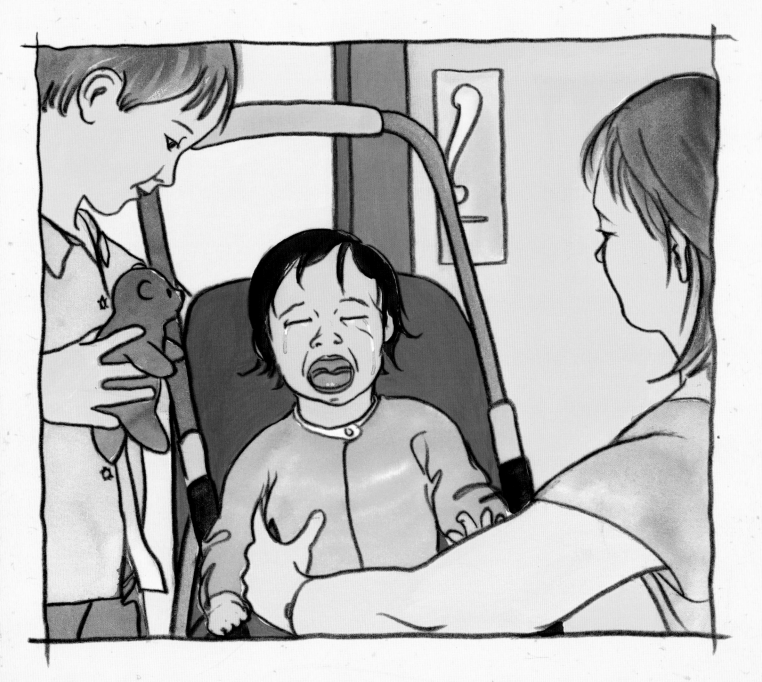

It is a whole day of crying. We try out all the toys we brought for her. We try to give her cookies and a bottle. Dad holds her, Mom holds her, and we show her the TV. She screams whenever I try to hold her. She falls asleep in the stroller but cries again as soon as she wakes up and looks at us. Mom says that for May, this whole thing is a big surprise, and that she needs time to understand what is happening. May is confused and scared, and I guess I can see why she would cry. I just wish she could see how hard we are trying to make her happy.

It gets dark, and I can hardly wait to go to bed and forget about it. But then she notices that the buttons on my shirt are shaped like little turtles. Finally, she likes something. She climbs into my lap and plays with the turtles for a long time.

My mother smiles and starts to lift her up for bed. But May gets a good grip on my shirt and holds on. She smiles for the first time. We all laugh, because we know she wants to stay with me.

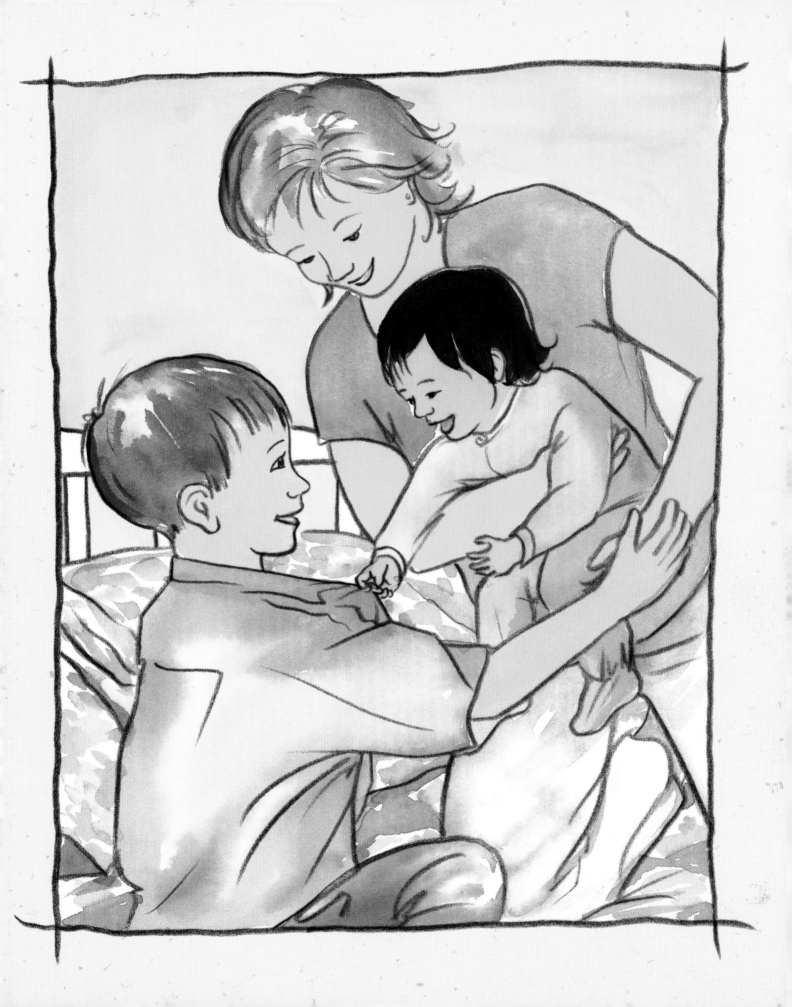

And I don't mind that at all.
In fact, that's what I've been waiting for all along.

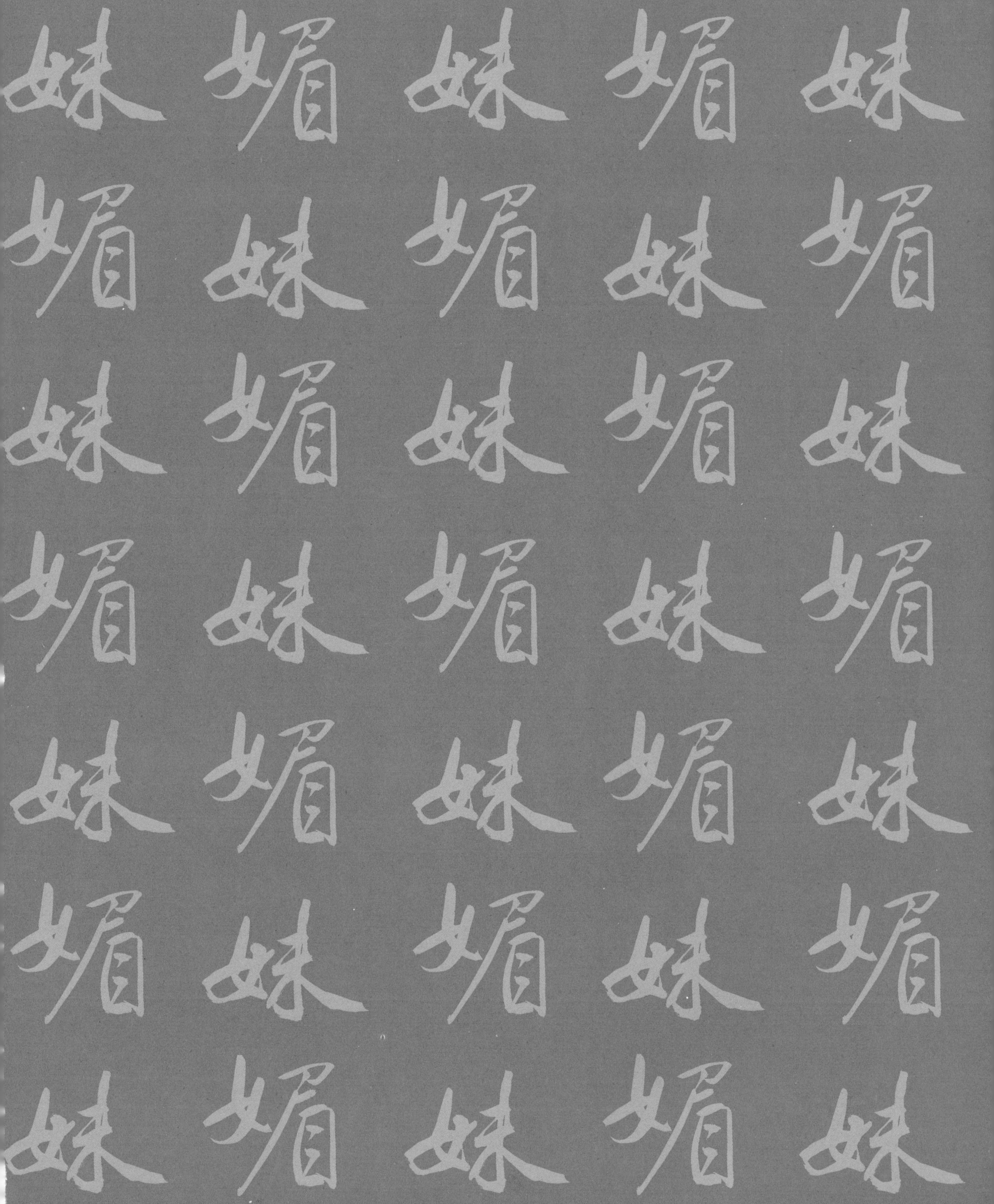
妹媚妹媚妹
媚妹媚妹媚
妹媚妹媚妹
媚妹媚妹媚
妹媚妹媚妹
媚妹媚妹媚
妹媚妹媚妹

OCT 2005